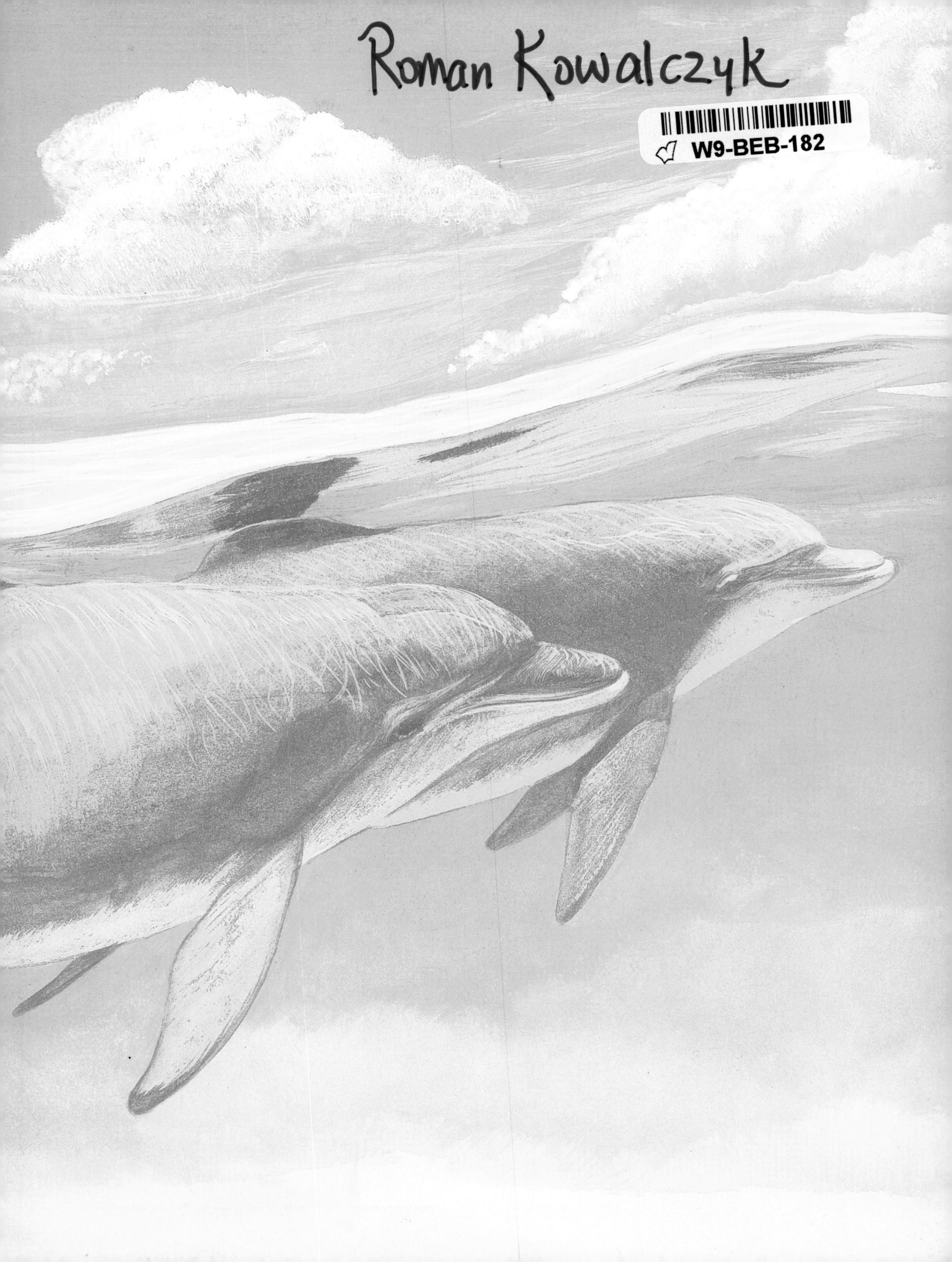

WE ARE
DOLPHINS

MOLLY GROOMS & TAKASHI ODA

For my pod, family and friends
who have supported and inspired me.

$\mathcal{B}$elow the water's surface, something magical was happening.

Around the cove, soft waves brushed the shore and gently rocked Mother Dolphin and her newborn calf as they rested. Little Dolphin blinked her large eyes several times as they adjusted to the bright light. Sunbeams shone down through the water, and the seaweed below swayed gently in the current.

Ready to help Mother Dolphin and her new baby, Aunt Dolphin gently raised the little calf to the water's surface.

Mother followed them and took a deep breath of air in through her blowhole. "You will need to take a deep breath, little one," she coaxed, as her baby tried to take her first breath. Little Dolphin coughed and spluttered until Mother showed her again.

At last, she drew in a deep breath, and her body

lightened and began to float. "Look, look! Mother, look!"

she squeaked. Little Dolphin was floating on her own!

"There you are, my strong little one," said Mother Dolphin. "You've learned the first skill of a grownup dolphin! You are very quick, indeed."

Little Dolphin squeaked again. Her voice bounced off and around the rock walls of the cove. "Oh, Mother! Did you hear me? Listen, it's me!"

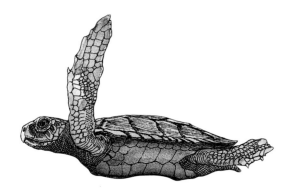

Mother Dolphin nuzzled her baby with her long beak. "Very good. You have just learned another important lesson. You have your very own voice, just as I have mine. Every other dolphin in our pod has a special voice as well. We will be able to hear each other even when we cannot see each other and are very far apart. You can sing to any other dolphin and use your voice to find out where you are and what you are seeing. That is what dolphins do."

"We are singers."

"Do you feel strong enough to swim?" asked Mother Dolphin. "Use your tail to push yourself through the water. Use your flukes to balance and keep upright. Your tail will also help direct you." Mother nudged her gently with her beak. "I will be right here with you."

Little Dolphin moved her tail slowly, and began to drift forward. Soon, she was swimming very quickly.

Nearby, the rest of the pod gathered and swam around Little Dolphin. Little Dolphin and another calf swam side by side. They chased each other in and out through the pod. Each swam faster and faster.

"Mother, we swam so fast!" she squeaked.

"We dolphins can swim very fast, indeed," Mother Dolphin replied. "We can swim fast enough to catch a school of tasty fish. We can even swim fast enough to race ships, and we usually win! That is what dolphins do."

"We are racers."

Just then, Little Dolphin spotted what seemed to be a cloud in the water ahead of them. "What is it?" she whispered to Mother. "Lunch!" said Mother Dolphin, and she began to swim so quickly that Little Dolphin could not keep up with her.

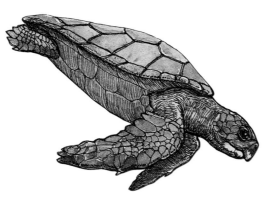

A school of shimmering herring zigzagged along in front of the pod. The older dolphins began to circle around the fish, driving them up toward the surface as the young dolphins watched.

The adults began to dart in and out among the surfacing school, snatching up mouthfuls of herring.

After she had filled her belly, Mother Dolphin returned to her calf. "Soon, you will be able to chase, catch, and eat fish just like that! Until then, you will have your mother's milk. Someday I will teach you where all the fish hide and how you can trick and surprise them. That is what dolphins do."

"We are fishers."

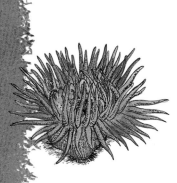

Suddenly, Mother and the other adult dolphins stopped and sang out warnings. Mother Dolphin gently pushed Little Dolphin toward the center of the pod. From inside the pod, Little Dolphin kept her body very close to Mother's.

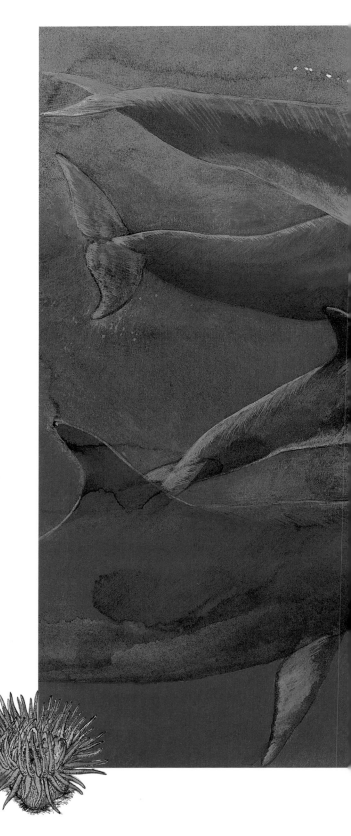

A large shark appeared. It was twice as big as Little Dolphin! It swam around and around the pod of dolphins, all the time watching them. The dolphins began to make more and more noise. Soon, the shark turned away and slowly disappeared.

Mother Dolphin reassured Little Dolphin, "We will always keep you safe from sharks and other dangers. We are much faster swimmers than any shark. We are also smaller, and that lets us move more quickly and easily. In the pod you will always find safety. That is what dolphins do."

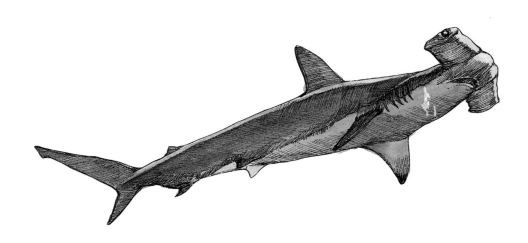

"We are protectors."

The pod moved back into safer waters nearer the
shore of the cove.

Swimming next to her calf, Mother Dolphin asked,
"What do you see below you, little one?"

Little Dolphin slapped her tail and dove to the
bottom.

The ocean floor was covered with starfish, beautiful pebbles, anemones, and colorful waving seaweed. The sun shone down through the water and cast shadows here and there among the rocks and plants.

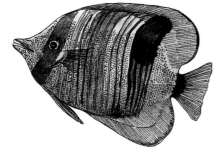

"There are more colors than I have eyes to see!" Little Dolphin exclaimed.

Mother Dolphin explained, "You can reach it any time you please, my little one. Dolphins can dive great distances. We can also stay underwater, holding our breath, for a very long time before we need to come back up to the surface to breathe. That is what dolphins do."

"We are divers."

Mother Dolphin picked up a shell from the ocean floor and swam fast. Little Dolphin chased her. Mother Dolphin dropped the shell, and then raced to catch it just before it touched the sandy bottom. Mother and Little Dolphin repeated this game over and over again.

"You and I will always enjoy playing with each other," Mother Dolphin said. "You will always be my little one, and even when you are all grown up, we will still play together. Because that is what we do."

"We are players."

We are singers.

We are racers.

We are fishers.

We are protectors.

We are players.

"We are dolphins."

NorthWord Press
5900 Green Oak Dr
Minnetonka, MN 55343
1-800-328-3895

Library of Congress Cataloging-in-Publication Data on File

ISBN: 1-55971-814-5

Printed in Belgium

10 9 8 7 6 5 4 3 2 1